Brandy
A Bliss Bay Romance
Kayla Love

Corner of Press

Chapter 1
A Blast from the Past

"**Y**ou've got to be fucking kidding me!" Brandy muttered under her breath. She looked at her reflection in the bathroom mirror and shook her head jostling her shoulder length black curls. She closed her wide, expressive brown eyes and let out a deep breath before shouting back to Melissa, who was in the kitchen of their shared beach house.

"Oh that Justin. Yeah, I know him through my childhood friend, Kevin."

Justin Jameson.

Brandy had *finally* managed to get Justin out of her daily thoughts a few months ago. Nearly a year after their whirlwind romance.

Justin Jameson.

As Brandy applied a layer of sunscreen to her caramel colored skin, her mind floated back to the moment when she met Justin Jameson.

It was Kevin's epic 30th birthday bash - a pajama party at a hotel! Kevin and Brandy had been friends since 7th grade, so it was a no-brainer for her to hop on Amtrak from New York down to Philly to celebrate.

At the party, Brandy rocked a hot pink silk pajama set a la TLC's "Creep" video. She felt good and knew she looked fly! She worked the room, per usual, chatting and laughing with friends, her signature vodka soda in hand. From gossiping with her high school crew to catching up on job promotions with a couple of Kevin's fraternity brothers, Brandy was having a blast! She was in the middle of a conversation with her friend Ryan when her eyes locked with those of a handsome man across the room.

Justin Jameson.

Her brain tuned out whatever Ryan was saying and her mind started racing. *Who is that?! I've never seen him before. OMG. He is ca-ute! I need to figure out how to talk to him.*"

"So, we'll see!" Ryan's voice interrupted her thoughts. She'd missed most of what he said, but figured well wishes would suffice. "Well, good luck with that! Good to see you, Ry!"

She made a beeline for the bar while keeping her eyes peeled for the handsome stranger. She loved her friends, but she had a new agenda now...

"Ketel and soda please!" she asked the bartender while her mind raced. *Seriously though. How have I not met this guy? I could have sworn I knew everyone in Kev's crew!*

It happened again. Brandy's deep brown eyes connected with the piercing blue ones of the hottie. She gave him a smile before turning to grab her drink from the bar. As she turned back around, he'd moved from the spot.

Dammit, Brandy! No excuses! Next time you have to make a move!

Thirty minutes of party passed and then finally, it was as if Moses had parted the Red Sea! There he was. It was like a gravitational pull that landed Brandy within his orbit.

"Justin," he said, extending his hand while maintaining eye contact. A chill went down Brandy's spine.

"Brandy," she said, firmly gripping his hand and offering her megawatt smile.

It was as if nothing else even mattered in the room, but the two of them. The party swirled around, but they only had eyes for each other. As they talked about everything and nothing, their bodies were drawn to each other like magnets and they found ways to touch. Like Justin brushing the small of Brandy's back as she sauntered by on her way to the bathroom and like Brandy gently grazing her nails against Justin's forearm as they waited at the bar for drinks.

An hour later, they had snuck away to a dark corner of the hotel bar where, in their tipsiness, they thought they were invisible to the rest of the partygoers. Wrong! (As they found out the next day when their makeout session was the talk of the morning after.)

After an intense liplock, Justin pulled away slightly and asked with a sexy smirk, "Wanna get outta here?"

Brandy smiled coyly as she looked up and made bedroom eyes with him. "Your place or mine?"

Brandy's walk down what was about to be a very sexy memory lane was interrupted by Melissa exclaiming, "Ready?!"

"As I'll ever be," Brandy whispered.

She shook her head in disbelief, yet again, as she followed Melissa out of the door and toward the beach. What were the odds that her old fling would be crashing into her orbit again?

Chapter 2
Remember Justin?

Through her Black Ray Bans, Brandy watched the aqua waves creep up on the sand. The sun was shining bright and there was a light breeze. It was a banner beach day. Brandy took in a deep breath of salt air and felt relaxed until the jolt of reality hit that she would be seeing Justin tomorrow. Only an hour before, Melissa casually dropped the news that Justin, her Justin (well, not actually her Justin, but her Justin) would be here. In Bliss Bay. Her quaint little beach town where she escaped most weekends of the summer.

How?

Well, as she learned, in the time since Justin disappeared, he'd met Melissa's friend, Kelly. He was home visiting his parents and met her at the gym. They started a whirlwind relationship, which led to him moving back to Philly from D. C., and in with Kelly, and now they were coming to visit Melissa at the beach house.

What are the odds?! What are the fucking odds?! Brandy mindlessly flipped another page of the latest edition of *Essence*. (As much as she was a modern woman all about her devices and apps, she still subscribed to a couple of print magazines and still refused to read books on an e-reader.)

Does Kelly know about me? I don't think Melissa does based on how she brought it up. And that means she doesn't know either. Ugh. And I can't tell her.

Melissa was a friend, but a newer friend she'd met here in Bliss Bay. Clearly, her allegiance would be to Kelly if anything went south.

Brandy's brain was on overdrive. She gave up trying to focus on an article about a woman who found her long lost family through a DNA test. She had her own drama to deal with! She had to talk to someone about this. As the sun warmed her back, she stretched over to her beach bag and pulled out her phone. She opened up the group text with her college girlfriends scattered across the country.

"OMG. You will *never* guess what's happening here. I mean never!"

"What?!" Danielle chimed in first. Danielle was Brandy's roommate for 2 years in college, who now lived in Baltimore, and was always ready for a juicy story.

"Don't leave us hanging! Aren't you at the beach this weekend? Did you meet someone?!" added Jasmine.

"So remember Justin..."

"Girl, how could we forget? How you two met is still one of my favorite meet cutes!" Nicole had entered the chat.

"Anyway. I'm at the beach house this weekend. It's Melissa's weekend, too. So we're getting ready for the beach when she mentions her friends, a couple, are guesting in the house this weekend. The girl of the couple is her friend. And she thought I might know her LIVE IN BOYFRIEND because he's from my hometown." Brandy typed frantically. "So she mentioned the name Justin. Well I went to high school with at least 3 Justins so it didn't even phase me.

Then she said Justin Jameson. Y'all. I damn near passed out!"

"..."

Brandy waited for her friends to formulate their responses of shock and awe.

"Just catching up. I can't even! What are the odds, Bran? How are you feeling about that?" Ananda empathized. She was a therapist and the voice of reason in the group.

"Stunned, I guess," Brandy responded. "How am I supposed to even act? I definitely don't think Melissa knows about us so I need to at least play it cool with her. This girl is her friend after all!"

"Damn. Well we are here for you! We got you, Bran! Don't make me have to hop in the car and drive up there from Baltimore!" Danielle exclaimed. And Brandy knew she was only half kidding. She was that kind of friend.

"Thanks, D. I'm okay. I will be fine! I will just be my best fabulous self!" Brandy exchanged a few more pleasantries with her friends and then returned her phone to her beach bag. If she was going to survive this encounter, she at least needed a beach nap! She drifted off thinking about the rest of that infamous night with Justin.

They decided to meet in Brandy's hotel room. She'd sneak out of the party first and he'd follow in 5 minutes. Brandy knew he was watching, so she sashayed out of the room. Let him know what he'd be working with!

She took the elevator up to her room on the 9th floor. She threw open the door and hurried to the bathroom for a quick freshen up. She knew the countdown was on, so she unbuttoned another button on her pj set revealing her ample cleavage barely covered by a sheer black bra. She spritzed a little perfume behind her ear just as there was a slow knock at the door. She cracked it open.

"Hey," he said as his eyes traveled the length of her body.

"Hey yourself!" she said as she opened the door further to invite him in. She put the 'Do Not Disturb' sign on the handle before closing and locking the door.

In mere seconds, Justin's hands were running through Brandy's curls as he planted kisses on her collarbone. She let out a soft moan as his hands traveled further down and lightly squeezed her ass. They stumbled toward the bed where Brandy decided to take control and straddle Justin on the edge of the bed. She tugged at his hair as she teased his lips with her tongue. Then, she slowly peeled off the robe he was wearing as a part of his costume revealing his muscular chest. She rubbed her hands up and down over his smooth skin causing him to shudder with excitement. That wasn't the only way she knew he was excited either! She could see it clearly through his boxer briefs. As she pulled away from his mouth, he took the opportunity to stare at her lustfully and slowly unbuttoned the rest of the buttons of her top and pulled it to the floor.

"You still have too much on," he whispered.

"Let's take care of that then." She stood in front of him and slowly shimmied out of her silk pants. They dropped to the floor revealing her thong.

Justin admired her nearly naked body for a moment before pulling her back close. He rubbed his hands up and down her waist placing slow, warm kisses down her belly. He then laid her gently on the bed.

"You good?"

"So good! Don't stop!" she exclaimed.

He hooked his fingers into the side of her underwear and pulled them down. She fluttered her legs to help shimmy them down and off. He tossed them to the side before excitedly diving face first into her sweet spot. She shrieked with pleasure as his tongue explored every angle and crevice.

***

"Want to head back to the house for happy hour?" Another Melissa question snapped Brandy back to reality. "Jeremy texted me that he and Matt made it to the house and the rest of the crew is on the way."

"Sounds good!" Brandy said.

Back at the house, Brandy and Melissa were met with hugs, hot dogs, and Dark n' Stormys.

Their house's official cocktail of choice. Per usual, Jeremy was already shirtless manning the grill. And Matt was playing mixologist.

Brandy scarfed down the perfectly grilled hot dog. Guess all that worrying made her hungry! She paused and took a sip of her drink. Mmm.

"Impeccable!" she exclaimed.

"Cheers!" Matt touched his cup to Brandy's.

"Cheers!" she responded.

Still in her bikini and cover up, Brandy made her way to the side door and shouted over her back, "Gonna hop in the shower, but will make a salad and pick out the wine when I get out!"

She adjusted the water in the outdoor shower, stripped down, and hopped in. She had always processed her thoughts best in the shower (despite getting scolded multiple times as a kid about the water bill!). However, this shower was her favorite. Something about the warm water rinsing away the salt and sand with a backdrop of clear, blue, summer sky. As she lathered up, she took a deep breath and thought about how grateful she was for finding this little slice of paradise.

Chapter 3
Dating Disasters

The Beach House. It really was Brandy's escape from the hustle and bustle of Manhattan. It was kind of a fluke that she even found this place last summer. She'd still been getting over a series of unfortunate dating events.

There was Kyle. The cute, blond investment banker who started off strong, but two months in pissed Brandy off with his lack of nuance when it came to intersectionality. He really tried to argue her down saying because Meghan Markle has money that her struggles and experiences with racism are less valid. Nah son! She couldn't be with someone that didn't get it, so they parted ways, and she put a pause on dating white men, and dating apps, for a while.

She got back in the saddle with JP. Also known as "abs" in the group chat. She met him at the dive bar at the end of her block. He was bartending there for the summer before heading to business school in Chicago. He was fun, fresh, and hot. Like a Krispy Kreme donut. And just as tasty! Mmm....But a woman can't live on donuts alone, so she went back to searching for substance.

She thought the third time would be a charm with Ben. They hit it off over red Solo cups of jungle juice at a birthday party. But after a string of sporadic dates, inconsistent phone calls, and random texts, he eventually stopped reaching out. Ugh. It stung. She knew she should have cut it off after the first time he canceled their date last minute, but in true Brandy form, she ignored the red flags and doubled down on being "perfect," engaging, and fun. She felt like if she worked hard enough to show him how amazing she was, he would improve his behavior and change. Nope. Like with all the other avoidant, inconsistent guys she picked, it ended up the same way - with her ego bruised.

And here she was again. After yet another short lived romance, almost 30, and all alone. Meanwhile, her friends seemed to be easily falling into long lasting relationships. It was like everyone else was getting into the VIP section of the club, but her! It was depressing. She decided that maybe she needed a reset.

But then, a month later, with no expectations but having fun with her friends, there was Justin.

Justin Jameson.

And everything changed! After their hot and heavy evening, they had a hotter and heavier morning! When they finally came up for air, hair disheveled, skin damp, Justin looked over at Brandy and asked, "Brunch?"

"Yessss. I could go for a plate of bacon and some coffee!" she replied as she sat up on her elbows. "Quick shower first?"

"Together?" he said, raising his eyebrows.

"Meet you in there!" she said and hopped out of the bed toward the bathroom.

They snuck out of the hotel without any of the other partygoers seeing them. They continued to get to know each other over bacon and bloody marys at Continental where they sat ridiculously close to each other.

"What time do you have to get back to New York?" Justin asked.

"Wellllll…my train is scheduled at 2, but I coulddddd be convinced to take a later one." Brandy offered.

"Tomorrow, late?" he whispered in her ear.

"I think that can be arranged," Brandy replied as she planted a kiss on Justin's lips. She took out her phone, and rescheduled her train. She'd cut it close in the morning, but she'd have just enough time to change clothes at home and make it into the office.

And thus began their whirlwind romance! Weekends back and forth between Philly and New York. Multiple texts throughout the week. It was everything Brandy dreamed it would be. Until it wasn't.

It started with less frequent texting and calls. Brandy assumed he was just busy so she didn't say anything. But then, on a Friday about a month and a half later, Brandy was preparing for Justin to come up the next day. She was feeling frisky after her lunchtime wax appointment and sent him a text.

"Hey hot stuff. Can't wait to see you tomorrow! Really. I can't wait for tomorrow. Why don't you come earlier? ;)"

A few minutes later, she heard back from Justin. "Yeah. How about 9?"

"Perfect! I'll be here. See you soon."

Brandy did a little dance as she walked up the steps of her building. When she got in, she took a shower, changed into her silk pjs, and lit a few candles. She wanted the mood set for Justin's arrival. She made a mini cheese plate, poured a glass of Cab Franc, and turned on *Real Housewives* while she waited. She looked down at her phone a while later.

9:12. *Huh?* Maybe Justin just hit traffic in the cab up from Penn Station. It was Friday night after all.

Another 10 minutes passed and no Justin. Brandy sent a text. "You good?"

What the hell is going on? This wasn't like Justin. He usually was more responsive. Although lately he'd fallen off a bit compared to the start of their relationship.

Her anxiety went into overdrive. *Maybe there was a train accident?* She opened Google on her phone and typed in "amtrak train accident." The results only revealed a story from 3 years ago.

Maybe she should call. She pressed send on his number and listened to the ringing.

No answer.

She started pacing the room. She pressed send again. Her heart was racing. Finally, she heard him pick up. *Okay. He's not dead. But since he's alive, WTF?*

"Hello? Brandy? You okay? Just seeing your text and missed calls." Justin shouted into the phone. Brandy could hear music in the background. *Wait, what? Why did he sound like he was out when he was already supposed to be here?*

"Uhh...I guess. You were supposed to be here at 9."

"Yeah. I will be. 9. Tomorrow morning..."

"Oh. Because when I said I couldn't wait until tomorrow that meant tonight."

"Aw shit. Yeah, no. Tomorrow. Listen, I gotta get back. I'll see you in the morning."

"Ok. See you then."

Brandy couldn't help but be disappointed, but it was just a misunderstanding and they'd have a great rest of the weekend. She clicked *Real*

Housewives back on and poured some more wine.

The next morning felt like deja vu. It was just after 9 am and Justin had yet to arrive - or reach out. Brandy poured some coffee...and waited. At 9:24, she sucked it up and gave him a call.

"Hello..." he answered sleepily.

"Hello! Good morning!" Brandy said sarcastically. "Are you on your way?"

"Damn...I must have overslept. Shit...I will be up there soon. Promise. I got big news for you, too!"

"Ok." Brandy replied tersely. She knew if she said anything else, she would go all the way off and didn't want to do that. But she was planning on him being here by now so she could eat. She was definitely feeling the hangriness!

"So sorry. Getting up now. I'll text you when I'm on my way."

Justin arrived a few hours later. Brandy was steaming on the inside. Her perfect plan for the day was thrown off with his delay. She decided not to say anything and ruin the vibe. What would she even say that wouldn't make her look like a controlling bitch? She'd just get over it.

Over lunch, she learned why Justin was out so late the night before. He'd gotten a promotion and was moving to D.C. Which would add two more hours to their distance. She was excited for him, but feeling trepidation about where they would go from here. rather than ask about plans for their future, she just decided to play it cool and make the best of their weekend together. Little did she know at the time, it would be the last time she would see Justin...until the unexpected run-in at Bliss Bay.

Chapter 4
Finding Bliss in Bliss Bay

After Justin got back, he was caught up with his move to D.C. despite promising Brandy a weekend trip to Cape May. His texts became fewer and farther between. He didn't initiate any plans or offers to get together. The heat between them had turned cold. Brandy was crushed, but had too much pride to say anything directly. She made a few last ditch efforts via text and phone, but at some point just threw in the towel and accepted that Justin had moved to D.C. and out of her orbit. She was just pissed he was too chicken shit to just say that he wanted out instead of just fading out.

So there she was. Three weeks later. Still sleeping on her side of the bed. Only crying herself to sleep every other night. Moping around on Sushi Sundays (the tradition she and Justin started during their fast and furious time together). One night, with *Girlfriends* on in the background, she reinvigorated her search for summer shares. She had first gotten the idea over bagels in the break room when her office manager, and work mom, Diane, mentioned looking into a summer share. She'd done them many summers in her heyday and even met her husband, David, of 30 years there. The idea was seconded by her cousin Gabby who also had a good friend meet her husband there, too. Well, that was enough for Brandy to do some initial research!

She decided she wasn't the Hamptons type. Driving? Lines for the bar? Definitely NOT her scene. The Jersey shore towns didn't leave much to be desired either, despite her Jersey roots. A bit more searching revealed a cute little spot with an adorable dockside restaurant, an expansive beach, and a slew of summer shares - Bliss Bay. Before she could commit to any house, she met Justin and forgot about it. Until now. Three weeks before Memorial Day and three weeks after things had ended with Justin.

The multiple options had dwindled down to just two, but one seemed more like her vibe.

Looking for fun, interesting, active city dwellers to join our house in Bliss Bay. Our house hosts a fun group for the 28-38 age range. House sleeps 12. Amenities include food and booze, fresh linens, sunscreen, a hot tub, beach chairs and more. Two spots left. Meet our crew on May 4th at Vol de Nuit.

Brandy was curious. Sure, it was a little out of her wheelhouse. While her friends made jokes about her making friends wherever she went, it was much more her speed to spend time with people she already knew and loved. Electing to spend many of her prime summer Saturdays with strangers seemed like a risk. Would they be cool? Would she end up on *Dateline*? She tried to convince Nisha to go with her, but on the day of the meet up, Nisha had some sort of spreadsheet emergency to work out, so she had to bail. Brandy had a choice. She could go home, put on pjs, order Thai food, and watch reality TV, or she could go to the meet up. PJs were tempting, but she knew something had to change and what if this had the potential to be something really fun?

Turns out...it was! She got a good vibe from the folks she met and thought, *what the hell!* Normally measured, Brandy made the impulsive choice to immediately Venmo the money to Jeremy securing her spot. Escaping to the beach and away from reminders of her relationship with Justin seemed like the perfect antidote for her busted heart and bruised ego.

***

Brandy turned the water off and grabbed her towel. Yup. Going to that meet up was one of the best things she'd ever done. Finding this community had enhanced her life in so many ways. From throwing theme parties here at the house to happy hour back in the city, it had been the boost her social life needed. Her only wish was that one of these days she'd meet a new bae! But nope. Nothing. Nada. It had been seven months since she went on one half assed date. And here she was, less than 24 hours away from being faced with her blast from the past and his almost fiance, with no prospects in sight.

After dinner, Brandy poured a glass of Cab Franc, her favorite wine she discovered on her trip to France post-college graduation. She joined the group at the table for a round of Hearts, but her heart was only half in it. She managed to have a few laughs and win a hand or two before excusing herself from the table.

"Where you going, B?" Melissa asked.

"Eh. It was a long work week. Going to take it down." She poured another splash of wine into her glass. "I'll catch you tomorrow."

Brandy walked to her room and gently closed the door. Putting on that "everything is okay" act was exhausting and she just needed some alone time. The truth was she was sick of being single. Tired of two month relationships despite her best efforts. And knowing she was facing a part of her past tomorrow just rubbed salt in the wound. She slipped into pajamas, crawled under the sheets, and glanced at her phone. She stared at the Facebook icon and bit her lip.

"Should I or shouldn't I?" she thought out loud.

She'd played with the fire of snooping on love interests in the past and always gotten a little singed. What would she have to gain by seeing the journey of Justin and Kelly through their selfies and milestone posts? Nothing, but loss of sleep! She plugged in her phone and turned it over. She picked up her novel from the bed stand, took a sip of wine, and got lost in the story line to distract her from whatever was awaiting her tomorrow.

Chapter 5
Ex at the Beach

The next morning, the sun poured in through the cracks in the blinds and touched Brandy's eyelids. She rolled over with a sigh and snoozed for another thirty minutes. She knew she had to face the day. So she might as well do it on her terms. She washed her face, brushed her teeth, and changed into her running shorts and a sports bra. She laced up her sneakers and stealthily crept out of the quiet, still house.

Everything and everyone had yet to be roused for the day. Once she was outside, she took in a breath of salty air, took a left, and headed down the tiny, carless path on her favorite run. Beyoncé blasted in her ears as she glided along the path taking in the view of small beach cottages and the ocean in the distance. She attempted to think about possible scenarios of the pending run-in, but eventually quit. It was going to go how it was going to go. She resigned herself to this fact by the time she wrapped up her run. She was a hot sweaty mess. She didn't want to see Justin the first time looking like this, so she put some pep in her step and made her way back toward the house.

As she opened the door, she caught a whiff of her favorite Saturday morning scent: sizzling bacon and hot coffee.

"Morning, B! Good run?" Melissa asked as she poured herself a cup of coffee and picked up a slice of bacon from a plate.

"Yeah. It's getting hot out though," Brandy added as she grabbed a mug from the cabinet and poured her own cup of coffee.

"Nice. I can't wait to get to the beach. I'm going to wait for Kelly and Justin. They should be here in about 45. You wanna wait, too?"

Fuck. She couldn't really say no without it being weird. Well, at least she knew when the moment would be.

"Yeah. Sounds good." Brandy stuffed a piece of bacon in her mouth to keep her from blurting out anything she didn't want to say.

After finishing her eggs, another piece of bacon, and some avocado, Brandy hopped in the shower. If she was going to have this run-in, she was going to look damn fine! She pulled out her hottest bikini - jungle print and stringy. She took a glance at herself in the mirror. Yupppp. She was serving, "don't you wish your girlfriend was hot like me" vibes!

She was stalling in the room trying to figure out if she should be in her room when they arrived or out in the living room, casually reading a magazine, looking easy, breezy, and hot.

"Wish me luck, y'all. It's happening soon!" Brandy sent a text to her crew.

"I want the play by play. And good luck!" Jasmine exclaimed.

Brandy snapped a selfie in the mirror and sent it to the group.

"Damn girl! That suit is fire. You are fabulous and you got this! Just be your amazing self!" chimed in Ananda.

"Thanks, friends! Stay tuned..."

Brandy picked up her beach bag and prepared to leave her room when she overheard Justin's familiar laugh. Her heart fluttered. *Here goes nothing.*

***

Brandy emerged from her room with only a slightly forced smile. Melissa looked up from the cooler she was packing to take down to the beach. "Hey B! Look who's here!"

"Oh hey!" Brandy said with as much excitement as she could muster.

"Hey Brandy! How've you been?! Such a small world that we're here together this weekend," Justin said, a little too eagerly.

He must be nervous. He gave her a brief, awkward side hug before stating, "This is my girlfriend, Kelly. Kel, this is Brandy. Remember I mentioned she's a childhood friend of Kevin."

Well that's an interesting description. So, he's really trying to pretend like we are just casual acquaintances and not two people who've seen each other naked? Well, okay.

"Hey Kelly," Brandy said.

"Hi." Kelly gave a brief wave and then walked into the kitchen to help Melissa. Meanwhile

Brandy wondered, did she know? It was hard to tell. Maybe she was shy. Maybe she was "team no new friends" and just wanted to connect with Melissa.

And then there were two.

"Umm...so, it's a...hot one out there," Brandy said, forcing out the words. *The weather, Brandy? Really. You told this man about when you were bullied in 7th grade, but now the best you have is the weather?* She also noticed she was tapping her foot. *I guess I'm a little nervous, too.* She only tapped her foot like that when she was feeling anxious about something and needed to get out that energy.

"Yup. Uhh, that ferry ride was nice." Justin pointing in the direction of the bay. After an uncomfortable few seconds of quiet, he added. "Nice breeze."

"Yeah...." Brandy trailed off, looking away. She wanted to avoid eye contact with Justin. She knew if she looked directly in those piercing blue eyes, her heart would shatter at the thought of what was and what could have been. *I deserve an Emmy for playing it this cool!* She rustled around in her bag like she was looking for something, when really she was just looking for an excuse to not engage with Justin. When she took a quick look up, he was doing something on his phone.

The silence was cut by Melissa asking, "Ready?!"

"Yeah! Let's go!" Brandy exclaimed, putting on her Ray Bans and power walking toward the door. The foursome departed for the beach.

Down on the beach, they set up their area next to where Matt, Jeremy, and some other friends had set up shop. Brandy lathered up on some more sunscreen, grabbed a seltzer, and plopped down in her chair, with a magazine, the sun's rays warming her skin. Meanwhile, Justin took the task of putting up the umbrella.

"That's my strong man!" Kelly exclaimed in her saccharine sweet voice standing by. "Thanks, baby. You know I need the shade." Her pale skin was a stark contrast to Brandy's sunkissed caramel skin.

Behind her sunglasses, Brandy rolled her eyes and flipped the page. She put in her ear buds. Typically, she could barely get through a book or a magazine at the beach. She would try, but would inevitably end up in a conversation or playing Scrabble or something more interactive. But she needed to block out the fact that the man who left her hanging and hurting was just a few steps away.

About 40 minutes later, her reading of the article about the woman and the DNA test was interrupted by a tap on the shoulder. She took out her ear buds. "Hey B!"

It was Melissa. "We're going to hop in the water. Wanna join us? Matt said it was warm. I know you only go in then."

"True…but I'm okay, thanks," Brandy responded. "I'll hold down the fort." Brandy did indeed love when the ocean felt like bath water, but she wasn't interested in being around Justin and Kelly.

"Aww, you sure you're okay?" Melissa asked. *Eep.* Brandy wondered if she was showing her cards that something was off with her. She would have to fake the funk a bit better.

"Oh yeah. Next time! I'm just enjoying the sun and this magazine. Thanks!" she said, adding a little pop to her reply.

Melissa, Justin, and Kelly walked to the water. Brandy moved to her belly on the blanket and flipped to a spread on fall fashion with only the crashing waves as her soundtrack.

A short while later, Justin, Kelly, and Melissa came back. Kelly, walking back to her spot under the shade, dripped cold, salt water on Brandy, completely oblivious, which tap danced on Brandy's last nerve. One of her biggest pet peeves was when people were unaware of their surroundings. She was also grappling with just how different she and Kelly were. It was activating her insecurities about being chosen. *How could Justin go from this to that?*

As they sat back down, Kelly started talking to Melissa about how Justin had asked her to move in. Hot tears pricked Brandy's eyes. She was grateful for these sunglasses. Overhearing this conversation felt like a knife twisting her heart because it was everything Brandy had wanted and now somebody else had it! If she was honest with herself, there was definitely a moment when things were going well with her and Justin where she would let herself daydream about their future. How she would eventually move back to the Philly area for him. They'd find a cute place in Old City. Maybe get a dog. Eventually have a fabulous city wedding.

"So now we're figuring out how to decorate the office..." Kelly stated.

Brandy put her ear buds back in. It would be different if she had bounced back and found a new guy that she was planning a future with, but nope. The most interaction she'd had with a man was one lackluster date and the most action her nether regions had experienced was with her vibrator.

She pulled out her phone and sent a text to the group chat.

"Y'all. Take me out of my misery! Being around Justin is awkward AF. Talking about the damn weather. Ugh. And now the GF is talking about them moving in. I need a drink!"

Nicole was first to chime in. "WTF? Go do a shot!"

"Aww I'm sorry, B. That sounds stressful." A classic Ananda response.

"Not the weather! Ugh. Hang in there, boo!" Jasmine offered.

"So he had nothing to say about how he was an ass? Boy bye!" Danielle replied.

Before Brandy could fully close out her messages, another message popped up from Danielle just to her. "Hey B. How are you really doing?"

Her eyes watered again. Her best friend could see right through her text. She used her towel to wipe her tears, but pretended she was just dabbing the sweat from her face. She responded, "Honestly, it just really sucks. And the fact that he picked someone soooo different from me. Maybe I was just stupid for thinking it was ever going to work."

"Hey! Don't be calling my best friend stupid. But seriously, B, there was no way you could have known it would have ended the way it did. You are incredible just as you are. It's his fucking loss!"

"Thanks, D." Brandy closed her phone and then her eyes.

A while later, Brandy stood up and stretched. She wrapped her sarong around her waist, put on her flip flops and announced, "Heading up to the house. Anyone need anything?"

"Field trip! I want to come! I didn't want to go by myself." Kelly hopped up. The fiercely independent Brandy bit the inside of her lip to avoid laughing, or maybe screaming. This chick was really annoying. But maybe that was the silver lining of this situation. If this is the type of woman Justin wanted, it definitely never would have worked out for them in the long run.

"Can you bring back some rosé?" Melissa asked.

"Yup," Brandy responded and turned to walk toward the path toward the house.

"Baby, you gonna be okay? You need anything at the house?" Kelly asked. Brandy happened to turn around at the moment Kelly was caressing the back of Justin's neck. She quickly turned away and started walking. Her heart felt like it was beating out of her chest. She overheard Justin say no. Kelly chirped, "Here I come!"

The brief walk to the house felt like an eternity. Brandy racked her brain to think of some meaningless chatter to pass the time. They talked about Bliss Bay, the weather, and the evening's dinner plans.

When they got to the house, Kelly ran into the bathroom while Brandy grabbed some cherries from the fridge and put them in a bag to take down to the beach with the bottle of rosé and a few cups. Then, Brandy used the bathroom.

As she walked out, she noticed the house was silent. As she pulled her curls up onto the top of her head, she looked around and Kelly was nowhere to be found. *Oh. So she needed an escort up here, but not back. Okay.* She shook her head and scrunched up her face. She grabbed the bag with the refreshments and headed back to the beach.

As she approached the group, Kelly decided to announce, "Oh and, guys, Brandy was definitely getting all kinds of looks when we were walking up to the house! You should have seen it!" she exclaimed as she tapped Justin on the arm. "So many guys were checking her out!" At that moment Brandy made eye contact with Justin whose face was a mix of curiosity, concern, and recollection. "It must be because you have big boobs," Kelly concluded. "Well, they are legendary!" a stunned Brandy managed to quickly quip back.

Why don't you ask Justin about them?

Chapter 6
Brandy's Big Lie

B randy didn't really tell Kelly to ask Justin about her boobs. It certainly crossed her mind, but she wasn't going to blow the entire afternoon up for everyone. She refused to give Kelly the satisfaction of killing her vibe. This heifer should be grateful though. *And seriously, how could he have gone from this to that?*

In actuality, Kelly was, for the first time all day, rendered speechless at Brandy's "legendary" comment, while Matt, Jeremy, and Melissa gave a chuckle. Brandy could see a flush of red on Justin's cheeks out of the corner of her eye as she poured some rosé into the cups. He turned toward his book and pretended not to hear the conversation.

As the sun started to make its way toward the horizon, Brandy returned to the house for a quick shower and to start preparing dinner. It was her night to cook anyway, but it was a sweet relief to get some time alone. In the kitchen, she poured herself another glass of rosé, turned on some classic hip hop, and started chopping veggies.

The crew started to trickle in about an hour or so later for dinner. Brandy was so busy plating the shrimp tacos that she didn't have time to pick a seat away from Justin and Kelly at the table and ended up directly across from them.

Great...

"Well, we started redecorating the bathroom because somebody thought it was too feminine," Kelly said, teasing Justin. She took a chip, scooped some guacamole on it, and fed it to him. With that, Brandy chugged the rest of her margarita.

"Awww. I love it!" Melissa exclaimed. "You two are just the cutest!'

It was too much. Brandy got up to refill her drink and take a commercial break from the Justin and Kelly show. When she sat back down, Justin was talking about their debate over dog names.

"I mean, we have to decide soon, Kel. You're the one who wants to get him a custom sweater for the Christmas pics with my parents," Justin stated.

There it was again. That ache in the center of Brandy's chest. Photos with the family? That was next level serious. And so far away for Brandy in her life. All she could do to avoid the nagging at her heart was focus intently on her taco and its contents.

"Dinner was delicious, B! Thanks!" Melissa said as she started collecting plates to take to the kitchen.

"I'll help you!" Kelly stated as she only took her and Justin's plates. Not without planting a kiss on him on the way to the kitchen first.

While Kelly was in the kitchen with Melissa cleaning up post-dinner, Brandy found herself alone at the end of the table with Justin. The other end of the table was involved in an intense discussion about student loans and not paying them any attention.

"Hey. So..." Justin started before taking a quick look over his shoulder to see if Kelly was still in the kitchen.

"She doesn't know, you know," Justin blurted out quickly in a hushed tone. "About us."

"I figured," Brandy replied evenly, attempting to play it cool. She wondered if that response appeared too terse. After a beat she added, "I'm not going to say anything, of course. And I haven't said anything to Melissa."

There. That was mature, not bitchy, not emotional. Back to winning my Emmy for this performance of cool, unbothered ex.

"Okay, thanks. I mean, I know it was a while ago and not that serious. I just know her so well. She'd definitely feel some kind of way and make the rest of this weekend uncomfortable...for all of us," Justin shared, nonchalantly.

Not that serious? Brandy thought, crestfallen and speechless, keeping her face as neutral as she could although she could feel the heat of rage in her cheeks. *I mean, no, we hadn't made things official official or moved in together or planned on getting a pet, but damn. We had spent a lot of time together. I told him about my life, my goals, my dreams. How could he toss it away as if it meant so little?*

"Well..." Brandy started to say when she was interrupted.

"Babeeeee. Here's another Corona for you!" Kelly said as she plopped down next to Justin and put a beer in front of him. "What are we talking about?"

"Margaritas," Brandy answered as she stood up from the table. " And on that note, I need to fill mine up again."

***

Later that evening, the crew was sipping cold Coronas at the local bar, The Sand Dollar, when Kelly begged Melissa to go pick out songs in the jukebox. Justin wasn't a fan of pop songs, or dancing, so he wasn't interested, and was content to stand by the bar sipping his beer. Meanwhile, Brandy was chatting with some of her friends from another house. When she turned back around, it was just she and Justin standing there facing each other. She caught a whiff of his cologne that immediately transported her back to the first time she met him. She took a step back.

"Where'd Jeremy and Matt go?" she asked, wondering how much longer she'd have to be alone with him and pretend things were just fine. She feared if she stood here too long, the words would bubble up out of her and she'd go off on him. Not that serious...ugh. She was still pissed!

"Jeremy said it was 'lap time' or something like that and then they went that way," he answered.

"Oh. Okay," she said curtly. "Lap time" meant the guys were doing a lap around the bar to see who was out and about. She knew it would be a while. She took a long, slow slip of her beer.

Like on cue, Kelly and Melissa came bopping back, waving their arms in the air, and singing "I throw my hands up in the air sometimes!"

"It's shot o'clock, guys!" Kelly exclaimed and waved over the bartender. "It's on the Jameson tab."

Kelly, Justin, Melissa, and Brandy each threw back a tequila shot. "Yay!!!!" Kelly cheered and put her arm around Brandy like they were old friends.

Damn. This alcohol is hitting her. She's all of a sudden trying to be my BFF. I need to text the girls about this!

"Another round!" Kelly asked the bartender. After they licked, shot, and sucked, Kelly blurted out loud, "So...who do you have your eye on tonight, Brandy? Ooh he's cute over there!" She pointed in the direction of a guy on the other side of the bar. Brandy was mortified. There was no way in hell the girlfriend of her ex-whatever-he-was-to-her was going to try and set her up with someone.

"Oh, no one here. I'm seeing someone back in the city," Brandy blurted out before she could choke back the lie.

Shit! In the moment, it seemed like a quick fix to change the conversation. And pretend like she'd moved all the way on, since clearly, Justin had. She quickly realized how wrong she was.

"Really?" Melissa asked. "You've been holding out on us? When do we get to meet him?"

"Meet who?" Jeremy asked as he and Matt walked back up.

"Brandy's new guy!" Melissa exclaimed.

"Secrets, huh, B! Up high!" Jeremy exclaimed as he put up his hand for a high five. Matt did a little dance.

"Um, it's still new and all...." Brandy stumbled. Ugh. This plan was definitely going awry.

"What's his name? Tell us more!" Kelly jumped back in the conversation

"Your round!" Brandy was saved by the bell, well, rather the bartender doling out another round of shots. She definitely needed one to avoid this awkward AF conversation.

Chapter 7
The Helpful Stranger

Brandy knew she needed to escape ASAP. Tequila was her truth serum and she couldn't imagine backtracking this damn lie she just told. Especially in front of Justin! Fortunately, at that moment, the opening notes of Katy Perry's Firework started and Kelly grabbed Melissa's hand and went skipping toward the dance floor to bust a few off beat moves. Now normally, Brandy was the diva of the dance floor, but tonight wasn't the night. She didn't want to be in this awkward situation anymore. Plus, Kelly might start a cat fight if she's embarrassed off the dance floor!

Maybe there was a way out of this mess. Brandy could get Jeremy and Matt alone and let them know the real deal. But how? Justin wasn't a big dancer, so he'd posted up at the bar with the guys. Maybe when he went to the bathroom. All that beer he was drinking, he'd need to go soon, right? And he wasn't going to drag the guys along with him. Brandy would just bide her time.

She pretended to be really into the conversation the guys were having about baseball. She didn't love baseball, but she could keep up with the conversation, thanks to growing up watching with her brother.

Finally, Justin excused himself to go to the bathroom. Now was her chance! She started, "So uh...about earlier."

"What's that B?" Matt asked as he held out a $20 bill toward the bartender in an attempt to get some more drinks.

She spoke a little louder. "I was saying. About earlier, when I mentioned the guy..." Before Matt could respond, cheering erupted from behind them. They turned around. Some guys were in a dance battle! She turned back toward Matt just as Justin walked back up. *Well, there goes that chance.*

A few moments later, Brandy thought she had another opportunity. Kelly had waved Justin over to the jukebox and he reluctantly walked over. She was alone with Jeremy and Matt. "So tell us more about your new boyfriend!" Matt teased.

Brandy took a nervous sip of the Ketel and soda she'd switched to, ready to fess up. "Well, actually..."

"Give me everyyyyythingggg tonighhhttt!"

Brandy recognized Melissa's off-key voice. Another chance thwarted. She could also feel herself getting tipsy, which always led to her losing her usual filter. She had to get out - and now!

"Going to the bathroom!" Brandy said. Instead, she slipped out of the side door of the bar without being spotted by anyone she knew. She didn't want to deal with the pleas to stay. She thought about going to her favorite peaceful place on the bayside dock, but with the sounds of Rihanna trailing behind her, she changed direction and walked the three short blocks over to the other bar in town, The Bungalow, in search of a distraction.

She spotted an empty seat at the bar and sat down with a sigh. What was it about being around Justin and Kelly all day that brought out this side of her that wanted to compete and compare? When she admitted the truth to herself, she realized this wasn't about Justin. Or Kelly. It was about her.

It was about that empty space in her bed - and her heart. Seeing Justin and Kelly just reminded her of what she wanted and had struggled to find. She just wanted to be chosen by one of the good guys! The apps were painful and she just wasn't going to give it up for a dude with a dirty bathroom selfie or someone who couldn't form a full sentence. It was depressing.

She shook her head, "I still can't believe I did that."

"Excuse me?" the guy to the left of her said.

"Huh?" Brandy replied.

"You said something. Thought you might be talking to me."

Brandy realized she had actually said her thought out loud. She did have a habit of talking to herself. At about that time, the shots started to hit a little harder.

"Ah sorry! I thought I was talking to myself. But since you asked...I basically got myself in a situation."

"Do tell," he stated. She noticed his adorable dimple as he smiled at her and took a swig of his beer.

"Let me get my drink first and I will." She didn't need another drink, but dammit, she was going to have one!

She asked the bartender for a Ketel and soda, and then added an order of fries because she knew she was going to need something to soak up the vodka tequila soup swimming in her stomach. She then turned back to the handsome stranger who she now noticed was rolling solo.

"So..." she began as she turned her body to face him, bronze legs crossed. "I dated this guy for a couple of months last year. And we really connected! Or, so I thought. And because you can't make this shit up, can you believe he randomly ended up *here* this weekend? Not just here. Guesting in my damn house!"

She took a sip of her drink. "And not just alone, of course. That would be too simple. He's here with his LIVE IN GIRLFRIEND!" she said using her hands for extra emphasis. You can't take the Jersey out of the girl after all.

"And...she doesn't know about our past! So I'm having to be all fake-ity fake like, 'Oh yes, he and I have a common friend' and not 'Remember that one time, after the birthday party at the hotel...' It's just....a lot."

"Sounds like it," he said with a nod of his head, but otherwise, seemingly unphased.

"But there's more!" she said with a swipe of her arm.

"Not more!" he said, showing off that smile again.

"Oh get this!" she said lightly touching his forearm. "Me and my big mouth. So, I've been a wee little sensitive, I guess, about seeing this guy and being single. And it's been a longgggg, dry ass year since the break up and just being around them was just too much. Then, that chick was trying to find randoms in the bar to hook me up with! I just snapped. Well my version of snapped. I didn't do anything that crazy! And so before I realized it, I blurted out that I had a new guy back in the city. Fuck. Me."

He let out a chuckle. "Wow...um, what's your name? Don't think I got it."

"Sorry! Brandy," she said, extending her hand. He gripped firmly and shook. A tingle went down her spine. Was that a little electricity she felt between them or just all the alcohol? "And what's yours?" she said, batting her eyelashes a bit.

"Jalen."

"Nice to meet you, Jalen. And thanks for listening to my rant. Want a fry?" she asked as the piping hot plate and a bottle of ketchup were placed in front of her.

"So...what are you going to do Brandy who needs a fake boyfriend?" Jalen asked. He dipped a couple of fries in ketchup and placed them in his mouth.

"Well, that's the part I have to figure out..."

Chapter 8
The Morning After

T he next morning, Brandy woke up parched with a slight headache. She desperately needed water. And coffee. And some sustenance. A bacon, egg, and cheese on an everything bagel would be perfect right now. After all the alcohol she consumed, she was grateful she didn't throw up. Must have been the fries. At The Bungalow.

Ohhhhh. It was all coming back to her. The memories of the previous night came flooding back as redness came flooding to her cheeks.

So it wasn't a dream. She sure did get tipsy, make up a lie about a fake boyfriend, and tell the story to the guy next to her at The Bungalow! Ugh. What was his name again?! Her brain, fuzzy from the lack of nourishment, wondered. *Jared? Jason? Jaden?*

Jalen.

She picked up her phone and saw a text message revealing his name. Apparently, she held it together enough to get his number and name in her phone.

"Feeling ok over there, homie?" he asked.

She would respond in a bit. But first she had to put together the events of last night...

After she told Jalen the whole story, including the part about her sexless past year (cringe!), he asked her about her plan. She shared that her goal was to confess to Jeremy and Matt tomorrow. If she could get them alone. Laugh it off. Make like it was a joke. But let Justin and Kelly continue to think she has this fabulous boyfriend in the city. She likely wouldn't see them again any time soon anyway.

"But wait. What about the other girl?" Jalen asked.

"That...is the tricky part!" she said, shaking her finger.

"How 'bout this?" he began. "You need a cover? Holler. I took a few acting classes in college.

I bet I could be the Denzel of fake boyfriends."
He held his bottle of beer like an Emmy.

"I just might take you up on that!" Brandy
exclaimed with only a hint of a slur. "In that
case, you better start talking. I got a lot to learn
about you!"

Brandy fumbled around in her bedside draw-
er. She popped two Advil. She could smell coffee brewing. She almost went straight to the
kitchen, but recalled that Justin and Kelly might
already be in there. I mean, she may have told a
stranger all her business, but she still had some
dignity. She wasn't going to go out there with
raccoon eyes and her hair looking a mess. She
made a pit stop to the bathroom to put herself
together a bit. When she emerged, only Jeremy
was in the kitchen.

"What's up, B?" Jeremy asked. "Coffee?"

"Please!" she replied. Ooh. Maybe this was
her chance! It was just her and Jeremy in the
kitchen. If she could at least tell him...

Jeremy handed Brandy a mug of coffee.
"Where'd you end up last night? You weren't
leaving us to talk on the phone with your

boyfriend were you?" He jabbed like an older brother.

"No. Ugh about that though. So I was just..."

"I can't feel my face when I'm with you-uuu!" Melissa's off key voice filled the kitchen. Thwarted again! She really was going to have to call in this favor with Jalen after all.

Jalen.

Her mind flashed back to last night. She did at least ask him more about himself, like where he lived in the city (Brooklyn), why he was at the bar solo (sexiled by his roommate), and his favorite basketball team (Lakers).

He was sweet. Fun. And definitely a good guy if he was willing to help her out. And with all these thwarted opportunities to tell on herself, it was looking likely she'd need to call in the favor!

Indeed, she would. She never found a moment alone to reveal the truth. Not even on the ferry ride back to shore. Of course, everyone decided to ride the same ferry back as her and just had to sit together.

She spotted Jalen up ahead about to board the ferry as she and the crew lagged behind.

Shit! If he was going to be her cover, she had to pretend not to know him or see him. Even though she really wanted to stare at his dimples again. She decided to send him a quick text just in case.

"Hey Jalen! Hope you had a good rest of the weekend. Just in case I need to call in the favor, can you pretend you don't know me if you see me on this ferry ride? Thanks!"

She hit send. She watched as he felt the vibration of the phone in his pocket, took it out, read the message, and then turned around. Couldn't miss those dimples. He gave the slightest of nods as she raised her eyebrows at him without anyone else detecting.

As the crew sat on the top of the ferry, Brandy managed to drown out Justin and Kelly, one last time by pretending as if she was having a moment watching the sun making its way toward the horizon. She pulled out her phone and shot off a quick text to the group chat. "Y'all are never gonna guess what happened…"

Her phone vibrated with eye emojis, question marks, and people eating popcorn memes.

"So...I accidentally made up a fake boyfriend and now everyone wants to meet him...but then I met this other guy who volunteered for the job."

Her texting was interrupted by Jeremy's teasing. "Is that your guyyyy?!" Jeremy teased. Brandy looked up like the blank stare emoji.

"Uhhh...no," she stammered.

"Yeah right. What's up with being so secretive, B?! Is he famous or something?"

"No. No. Nothing like that. It's still early, you know."

"Well, I'll let you get back to your sexting!" Jeremy teased.

By the time she looked back down at the phone she had 34 missed messages. Damn, they typed fast!

"Girl, what?" Jasmine exclaimed.

"OMG, B. How did that happen?!" Nicole wondered.

"Wait, what happened with Justin and old girl?!" Danielle, and her aways inquiring mind, wanted to know.

"Short version is, I got all off my game because of old girl and then under pressure I...made up a fake boyfriend," Brandy admitted as she added a face palm emoji.

"You can't just say you broke up by the time you have to bring him around?" Jasmine asked.

"Good call, J. Maybe they'll find someone else to focus on," Brandy responded.

Brandy closed her eyes and took in the end of summer salt air as the ferry docked. Jasmine was right. She was just going to ride this out. Something else more interesting would come up with the crew and they'd forget about her fake man. She wouldn't have to embarrass herself by asking Jalen to be her fake boyfriend.

Once the dust settled, she'd tell the girls all about Jalen, but not yet. They walked off the boat and prepared to go their separate ways. Brandy was hopping on the shuttle for the train station while Jeremy and Matt were getting on the shuttle back to the East side of the city. Melissa was riding back to Jersey with Justin and Kelly.

"Bye!" Brandy said waving to everyone as she pulled her weekender bag over her crossbody style to avoid giving her usual hugs. Because if she started giving them out, she'd inevitably be forced to awkwardly hug Justin and Kelly.

"See ya soon, B. Post-Season Soiree?" Matt asked.

"Of course! You know I'm planning it," Brandy replied.

"That's right!" Melissa exclaimed. "Ooh, Kelly and Justin, you should come back up to the city for it!"

Fucccckkkkk. No! But she knew she couldn't say no.

"Oooh! That would be so fun!" Kelly exclaimed.

"Hope to meet your new boyfriend there, too!" Jeremy teased.

"Yes!" Matt interjected.

"Uhhh...ha ha...okay..." Brandy stammered with an awkward laugh as she climbed aboard the shuttle. Well, there goes the idea of a quick break up. Post-Season Soiree was in 2 weeks and that would be super suspect to break up by then. And plus, if Justin and Kelly were going to be there, she really needed to show up as the cool city girl with the hot guy on her arm.

She sat down and closed her eyes. She hadn't gotten herself in a situation like this in a while. She felt someone sit down next to her as she opened her eyes to send off a quick text to the girls. She spotted those dimples out of the corner of her eyes.

"Okay. Looks like we're doing this, huh? So what's the backstory? How did we meet?" Jalen said.

She smiled at him. "Hmmm....online? Produce aisle? Spin class?"

"Well, guess we better test those out this week so it can be believable, right?" Jalen said.

"Right," Brandy replied with a smile.

Chapter 9
Faking the Funk

Brandy started off the work week slammed. She hosted a panel for small business owners on Monday and then welcomed the new cohort of volunteers on Tuesday, so she was beyond ready for her monthly happy hour with Gabby. They had started this tradition when Brandy moved to the city five years ago. She always looked up to her older, stylish, and successful cousin.

Gabby was already at the table with the bottle of Prosecco popped when Brandy arrived. She stood up to give Brandy a hug as she said, "You see I took the liberty of getting the bubbles poured. I need this story! Spill it!"

Brandy shared the full story of the weekend as Gabby watched captivated. Between sips of Prosecco, she inserted "Oh no she didn't!" and "I would have wanted to cut her!" and "Awww!"

"So wait! You are hanging out with him on Thursday to create your fake first meeting?!" Gabby exclaimed.

"Yeah. We figured we would have some real moments to speak about, so maybe not a total lie?" Brandy revealed.

"OMG. I love it! Wait until I tell Dev!" Gabby shrieked. Dev was Gabby's boyfriend of four years. That she was not so patiently waiting to propose to her.

"Well, don't get too excited. It's just a two week thing to get me through this soiree and then we can have a fake breakup, I can save face, and move on with my life!" Brandy responded before draining her glass.

"We'll see! Maybe it will turn into something real!" Gabby, the eternal optimist and romantic, replied. "Don't hold your breath, Gab. I know I'm not."

***

On Thursday night, Brandy met Jalen after work at the Strand bookstore to test out a potential option for their fictional meet-cute. He was already there when she walked up.

"Hey," she said, a wee bit nervous as he greeted her with a hug. They were really doing this.

"What's up? How was your day?" he asked as he held open the door. "Good. We had a new cohort of volunteers start, so it's been busy."

"Gotcha. What do you do again?"

"Corporate Philanthropy. I lead our volunteer strategy."

"Okay, bet. We do a lot of volunteer programs at my company. I helped with Habitat for Humanity last year. It was really powerful."

"That's cool. So wait, what do you do?" Brandy asked as they wandered down the travel aisle. She pulled a book about Thailand off the shelf.

"Product Marketing."

"Oh cool. You like it?"

"I do."

Brandy and Jalen wandered the aisles. Each of them picking up a book here and there and asking the other a question. Travel. Ever been to France? Fiction. Have you read James Baldwin? Self-Help. Do you know your love languages?

"You hungry?" Jalen asked as he held the door of the bookstore open for her and she walked through.

"I could eat!" Brandy replied. "I can always eat, actually!' she said with a giggle.

"Okay. I see how you roll!"

They walked to a small, hole-in-the-wall place with the best Thai food Brandy had ever had in the city. Over green curry, she learned that Jalen had gotten his MBA at NYU, which brought him to the city after growing up in the Maryland suburbs, and undergrad at Morehouse. They ended up sharing more than one microaggression horror story growing up in very similar experiences being the only, the first, or one of the few. Time passed by effortlessly and before too long Jalen was walking Brandy to the subway.

"So I have it straight. We met on an app and then had this bookstore and dinner first date?" Jalen asked while waiting with Brandy on the platform for the A.

"Sounds believable enough to me! And thanks again, Jalen. I really appreciate it. See you Saturday?" Brandy asked as the automated voice indicated her train was arriving.

"Yes. Gotta get some Brooklyn content under our belts. Let me know when you get home, okay?"

"Will do," she said as she got on the train with a wave.

Brandy and Jalen had a whole schedule for the next two weeks. They planned a number of outings together to have some stories to tell at this happy hour. Then, Brandy would make something up to say they'd broken up a few weeks later, and then, they could go on about their lives.

Saturday morning, Brandy got up, threw on a yellow sundress and sandals, and took the 3 to Brooklyn on a perfect September Saturday, sunny and clear. Since she'd already met up with Jalen on Thursday, she didn't feel quite as nervous about their fake date today. She pulled open the door of the restaurant. Jalen was already waiting at the table. He stood up to greet her.

"Hey!" he said as he enveloped her in a big hug. The first thing she noticed was the scent of his cologne. It was warm and woodsy. She could also feel his strong, flexed biceps. She hadn't noticed that before. She noticed a tingling in her spine she hadn't felt in a long time.

They sat down and ordered two Bloody Marys, an eggs Benedict for him, a shakshuka for her, and a lemon ricotta pancake to share. They toasted to the day as the soulful sounds of jazz began to play. It was such a vibe! As the singer crooned "Someone to Watch Over Me," Brandy had to remind herself this was only pretend. Even though the soothing sounds made her want to reach across the table and grab Jalen's hand.

Girl! Don't get caught up. Take note for the stories and that's it. This is not your actual man!

After brunch, Jalen and Brandy walked over to the Brooklyn Museum to explore some of the exhibits and then a walk through Prospect Park. Damn. He's a cultured brother. She'd never really met anyone like him before.

He mentioned he had plans that evening so they wrapped their day after the walk. As Brandy rode the train back home she wondered what it would have been like to kiss Jalen's full, sexy lips.

It felt like an eternity getting to the following Tuesday night where Brandy and Jalen shared cocktails and stumbled into a karaoke bar. Jalen kicked off the night singing 'Poison' followed by Brandy singing 'I'm Every Woman' before they decided to do a duet together.

"What about 'Picture'?" Brandy suggested. "I called you last niiight at the hotelllll...." she sang while making a microphone out of her beer bottle.

"You really did grow up in the suburbs!" he teased. "I mean, I did too, and you know I know Sheryl Crow! But nah. I ain't singing no Kid Rock."

"Fineeeeee..." Brandy kidded. "Ooh. 'Heartbreaker?' I gotta skip the high notes though. I don't have that Mariah range!"

"Jay-Z I can do. Oh wait. Hold up," Jalen said. "Did you realize we are J and B? Aw shit! We gotta do "Bonnie and Clyde' then!"

"Yes! That's perfect!" Brandy grabbed the pen off the bar, wrote the code for the song, and handed it to the bartender.

Around 11 p.m., the duo called it quits. It was a work night after all. They confirmed their plans for Friday. Jalen hailed a cab for Brandy before heading home.

"Let me know when you get home, okay?" he asked as he held open the door for Brandy to get inside.

"I will," she replied. "Thanks for another fun night."

"Of course. We are going to have these folks convinced!" he responded as he closed her door.

On the ride uptown, Brandy thought about how much fun the past week or so had been. For a fake relationship, it was significantly better than some of Brandy's actual relationships! She had to remind herself this was just a two week agreement, not reality, and it was just a friend helping a friend. After next Tuesday, she'd be back on her own. But maybe, she should really think about getting back to dating again...

Chapter 10
An Unexpected Plot Twist

"**S**o....how's it going with the fake boyfriend?" Brandy read the text from Gabby on Friday morning as she sat down at her desk.

"It's coming along! It's actually been really fun. But Tuesday is the party so short lived."

"Does it have to be? I mean, it seems like you have a lot in common. Maybe it could become something real!" Gabby replied, excitedly.

Oh my hopelessly romantic cousin. Gotta love her. But my ass is too much of a realist. That sounds like something out of a rom com! "Life isn't like your Lifetime movies, Gab! And nothing has indicated that he's interested in anything more than friendship. Totally G-rated!"

"Well, you never know!" Gabby replied.

Brandy gave the message a heart and got to work. She had another fake date with Jalen later and needed to get a bunch of work done.

Later that evening, Brandy met Jalen for a movie. An action film he wanted to see. *See? Not romantic at all. If he was interested in something more, he would have picked a drama, or even a horror, in hopes of getting me to hold his hand or grab onto his arms. Those arms...*

After the movie, they stopped at a corner cafe and shared a slice of chocolate cake before heading toward the subway. A half block before the stop, they both heard iconic lyrics they both knew by heart.

"B-I-G-P-O-P-P-A!" Jalen sang while waving his arms in the air.

"No info for the D.E.A..." Brandy added with a little bop.

"Yo! You wanna go in?" Jalen asked with a grin.

"Don't have to ask me twice!" Brandy responded.

Jalen held open the door and Brandy walked through. Brandy grabbed them both beers and they moved to a small empty spot in the bar. As they drank, danced, and sang along to hip hop's greatest hits, the bar got progressively more crowded, moving Brandy and Jalen closer and closer to each other. It also got progressively darker as the music changed from hip hop to the sultry sounds of reggae.

It was then that Jalen reached for Brandy's hand, spun her around, and pulled her close from behind. As they began to grind and wind to the music, Brandy soaked it all in - the way his breath tickled her neck, how he held her close, his delicious scent. She realized it had been so long since she'd been this physically close to a man and how much she'd missed it.

Girl. It's just dancing! her mind said. But her body had a mind of its own! Her nether region tingled with desire to be rubbed, sucked, stroked. It had been far too long. She knew this was pretend, but damn it felt good. She also knew herself well enough that if he said the word, she'd be out of this dress in a flash. She had dropped her defenses.

"Sorry!" A random drunk girl shouted as she bumped into Brandy and Jalen breaking the spell of the moment. Brandy looked at Jalen. He held her gaze.

Everything in Brandy's body was pulsating. She wanted to jump his bones right here, right now, but what did he want? And she had to keep the end goal in mind, so she knew what she had to do.

"Umm... I guess we should get out of here," Brandy said.

"Yeah, okay." Jalen responded.

Brandy couldn't read that reaction. Was it business as usual? Did he want something more? What if he didn't and she made a fool of herself? But she didn't want the night to end. And in that moment, with that last drink Brandy felt bold. *What the hell? I should invite him for a nightcap. No big deal.*

As the cab Jalen hailed for her pulled up and he opened the door, Brandy turned back toward him.

"Hey," she started. "You wanna come back to my place for a nightcap? I have Hennessy." She knew Jalen loved Hennessy and she happened to have a bottle her brother had brought her when he came to visit a few months ago.

"Bet!" Jalen responded and climbed in the cab next to Brandy.

Brandy kept up the "just friends" ruse making small talk as the cab sped up the West Side Highway. It was quite the challenge. Their legs were touching. She could feel the warmth emanating from his body. It was all she could do not to reach over and grab his face and plant a hard, wet kiss on his mouth. Her mind also drifted to something else being hard and wet...

"84th and Columbus!" Her thoughts were interrupted by the cab driver announcing their arrival. They thanked the driver and departed the cab. Jalen handed him some cash while Brandy opened the front door. They walked up the steps to her 3rd floor apartment. When they arrived, Brandy grabbed two small glasses and poured the Hennessy.

"Cheers!" she said as she raised her glass to Jalen.

"Cheers!" he responded as he touched his glass to hers.

They both took sips of the warm, amber colored liquid. Brandy walked from the kitchen to the living room, only stopping to turn on some music. Jalen followed her to the couch. He was observing her intently as she told an animated story about her girls trip to Barcelona.

"So we ended up not getting back to the hotel until..."

Jalen interrupted her sentence by planting his warm, soft, moist lips on hers. He gently parted her lips with his tongue as he moved his hand to the side of her face, lightly rubbing his thumb over her cheek. Brandy's entire body felt electric. For a brief moment, she considered pulling away. They still had to get through Tuesday. *Would this fuck everything up?* But then she felt Jalen's lips making a trail from her lips down her neck to her collarbone. She let out a soft moan. Her body was turned on, so she turned off her brain and went with it!

As he continued to kiss her neck, he gently peeled the thin straps of her sundress down off of her shoulders, exposing more of her chest and revealing her cleavage. He continued to sprinkle her neck and chest with kisses as he reached behind and effortlessly unhooked her bra with one hand freeing her ample breasts.

"Mmmmm." Brandy noticed his devilish grin and that sexy ass dimple in his cheek. She arched her back toward him as he began to massage her breasts. "Uhhhhh..." she groaned as he replaced his dexterous hands with his deft tongue. As his tongue circled her nipples, she grabbed the back of his neck. Damn. This felt so good! As he made his way back up toward her lips, she decided to take control and straddled Jalen on the couch. She held his face with both her hands and kissed him hard on the lips before making her own trail down his neck. She could feel his excitement through his pants. He lightly tugged at her curls, which drove her wild! She couldn't resist. *Fuck it!* She pulled away only to grab him by the hand and lead him to her bedroom.

In the room, Brandy perched on the edge of the bed as Jalen quickly removed his shirt revealing his muscular chest and chiseled abs. She grabbed his waistband and pulled him close. She rubbed her hands up and down his muscular chest before gently tracing the outline of his abs with her index finger. She licked her lips seductively. Jalen laid her back on the bed, sliding her sundress off the rest of the way. He slowly kissed and sucked the trail from her breasts and down her belly until he reached her thong. He grabbed the material between his teeth and pulled the thong down to her knees before using his hands to take it off the rest of the way.

Damn. That was hot!

It got even hotter as Jalen found his way between her legs. She writhed in passion. "Ohhh! Ohhh!" she shrieked. Jalen moved his tongue even faster. She arched her back and held his head in the spot that brought her closer and closer to the edge. He continued to eat like it was the Last Supper! "I'm so close!" she exclaimed breathlessly. Within seconds, her body lifted up off the bed as she cried out in ecstasy before falling back on the bed in pure bliss. The usually verbose Brandy was speechless as she caught her breath.

When she could finally form some sort of sentence, she said, "That was...amazing."

"The pleasure was all mine," Jalen replied with a smile showing that dimple. "Although based on what I heard, I think the pleasure was also yours, too." He gave her a wink.

She giggled as she lightly hit him with a pillow. "Well, at least let me return the favor," she replied as she sat up and again pulled him close.

"Bet," he responded. She unbuttoned and unzipped his pants with a quickness before pulling down his boxer briefs revealing the excitement she'd felt earlier. Her eyes grew wide at the size of his erection. *Oh my! Better get to work...*

The next morning, Brandy could feel herself waking up, but kept her eyes closed. *OMG. I can't believe that happened. What am I going to do? I wish I could text the girls. I have to tell him this was just a one time thing, right? Just two friends having fun. Not 'I think I might be falling for you.' Shit! I'm falling for him.*

Brandy felt Jalen roll over in the bed. She was going to have to face the music soon. *Yes. I gotta get through Tuesday. I can't risk fucking this up now! I'll just play it cool.*

And that she did! She got up while Jalen still slept and freshened up in the bathroom. As she was pouring her coffee, he emerged from the bedroom. She offered him a cup of coffee, which he graciously took. She didn't want to give him any ideas, so she made it clear she had things to do today. Spin class, returning books to the library, happy hour with friends. Shortly after, he left and Brandy immediately hopped on the group chat.

"You will never guess what happened now!"

Chapter 11
The Other Woman

P er usual, the group chat was a wealth of knowledge, support, and entertainment. After the initial "get it girl" memes and eggplant emojis, she actually got some good advice from her girls. Get through Tuesday. Then reassess. And that was her plan...until Sunday.

Sunday morning after her run around the Reservoir, Brandy made a stop at the market. A black and gold label caught her eyes in the beer section. It was the 'Notorious' A.L.E. from a brewery Jalen had mentioned was his favorite. She'd never seen it at a store in the city before. She grabbed a six pack and decided she would give it to Jalen as a thank you gift. On her walk home, she thought it might be fun to go by and surprise Jalen with it later. Maybe they'd crack a few open and preemptively toast to a successful pseudo relationship.

Bzzzzz. Bzzzzz.

Brandy pushed the buzzer for Jalen's apartment. She'd asked him for his address a few days ago with the intent of sending him a thank you card. But here she was on his doorstep. When she texted him earlier, she'd casually asked what he was up to and he'd mentioned having a low key day at home, so she figured he'd be here and appreciate the surprise.

She heard the door click open. She walked through the double doors and up to the second floor landing. She knocked on the door with her free hand while holding the six pack and balancing a Levain cookies box in the other (she stopped by there on the way here). The door flung open and there stood a thin, Chrissy Teigen look alike in short shorts and a crop top.

Brandy felt the blood rush from her head to her feet and stumbled back just a bit.

"Ugh. Hi. I'm...looking for Jalen," Brandy said tentatively, while low key trying to peek into the apartment.

"Oh he's out now," the woman said, flinging her highlighted locks over her shoulder.

"Oh...okay. This is for him," she said handing over the beer and cookies. "Aw thanks, babe! How sweet! Are you his neighbor? Did he help you with something around the house? He's always doing sweet stuff like that...ooh Levain!" she said.

"No. Not a neighbor. Just owed him for doing me a favor," Brandy managed to eke out despite the lump in her throat. *Who was she? Why was she there half naked? Was he actually dating her? He had to be if she was there dressed like that!*

"Aww. Okay. Well, have a good day. Bye!" the woman said as she took a cookie from the box and shut the door in Brandy's face.

Tears started to stream down Brandy's face as she raced down the stairs. She couldn't even process what just happened. A *live-in girlfriend? He never mentioned that.* She knew this wasn't a real relationship, but she couldn't deny there was some chemistry between them. And the way he looked at her the other night. *Wait. So am I the other woman? Oh hell no! I'm no one's other woman!*

She yanked open the front door and as she prepared to walk through she slammed right into Jalen holding a take out bag of Shake Shack.

"Brandy?" he asked, surprised. "What are you doing here? You good? Oh shit, are you crying?"

Through her anger, frustration, and confusion she barely got out the words. "You...her...?" She shook her head. "Seems like you have a situation. So, umm. I'm good. And...forget about Tuesday. I'll figure something else out." She turned and started power walking down the block.

"Brandy. It's not what you think. It's not like that!" he yelled after her, but she refused to turn around and he knew he couldn't be spotted as a Black man running after a woman down the street without the potential for something to pop off. He stood there holding his bag trying to figure out how he could make this right.

Brandy slowed down a few blocks away. She ordered a black coffee and grabbed a stack of napkins at the bodega on the corner. She wiped her face and continued her walk toward the

Brooklyn Bridge. Was she really that bad of a judge of character? What kind of guy with a girlfriend volunteers to be someone else's fake boyfriend and go on fake dates? Had she totally missed the signs that he was unavailable? Not to mention - a cheater! What was she going to do? There was no way Jalen could be her fake boyfriend anymore. Not when he was living with another woman!

Through the random tears that kept falling (and that she kept wiping away with the bodega napkins), she frantically typed out the story on the group chat. "Y'all. What am I going to do?"

***

Brandy woke up in a haze with a slight headache Monday morning. She quickly remembered the events that transpired yesterday, including the multiple missed calls from Jalen last night and the very active, problem solving session on the group chat. Over the course of the evening, she acknowledged that: a) she totally had fallen for Jalen, so it was extra heart wrenching that not only had he lied to her, but he also had a girlfriend, b) she was going to have to make up a really good story or come clean at this happy hour tomorrow. Her thoughts were interrupted by another call from Jalen.

"This bold ass mofo!" she muttered. "Let me bless his soul!"

"Hello?" she said with a venomous force.

"Brandy! Please. Let me explain. I know it looks bad, but it's really not what you think."

"I've heard enough lies in my life. I don't need to hear some story, Jalen. You could have simply told me you had a girlfriend. I don't know why you would have agreed to help me if you had another woman waiting at home. That's just shady."

"She's not my girlfriend. Anymore. She's just staying there until the end of the month when she can move into her new place."

"Well, she seemed awfully cozy from what I saw."

She was met with silence.

"Listen, I need to run, so thanks, but no thanks. Your services are no longer needed. I'll figure this out on my own. Like everything else in my life. Goodbye, Jalen."

Click.

Whatever. Who has an ex just staying up in their house like that? She was not going to be made a fool. Well at least not by Jalen. She'd done enough of that over unworthy guys in her 20s. It really was too late to come up with a story. She was just going to have to face the music at the happy hour tomorrow and look foolish...in front of Justin.

The next day at work seemed to move at a snail's pace. She just wanted to get this over with. Brandy usually loved hosting the soiree, but her heart just wasn't in it today. She almost thought about pretending to be sick, but she did want to see some of her other friends.

The time passed and before long, Brandy was in a cab headed to the venue. In the back seat, she sent a final text to the group chat.

"Well, y'all. Here goes nothing. Time to come clean and look like a fool...sigh. Maybe this is the prompt for me to move to L.A..."

"You got this, girl! Just make it a joke. No need to get all emotional or give all the details! Make it like a delayed April Fools joke or something," Danielle replied.

"I'll report back," Brandy typed as the cab pulled up to the curb. She paid, got out, and thought, *here goes nothing...*

Chapter 12
Full Circle

When Brandy arrived, she could already see Jeremy and Matt through the window in the area they had reserved.

"Hey!" She mustered up as much energy as she could.

"B! Good to see you! Dark and Stormy?" Matt passed the drink to her.

"Hey Brandy! Where's the man friend?" Jeremy asked.

It was now or never. Regardless of who else showed up and when. It was time to come clean.

"So...about that. There is no man friend."

"What? You just don't want us to meet him!"

"No..." she said, taking a big gulp of the drink. "That was me. Making up a story. Honestly, it was an uncomfortable night. You wouldn't know this, and Melissa doesn't either, but...I used to date Justin."

Their eyes went big. Brandy continued. "A year and a half ago. It was a whirlwind and wonderful. Until it wasn't and he basically left me hanging. So it was just super awkward being around him and Kelly. And it was the first thing I could think of to make it seem like I was all good and moved on."

"Damn." Matt replied. "You could have told us, B. We would have your back!"

"Thanks, Matt. I know. I tried! But every time I tried it someone else came up or something would get in the way."

"So wait. You said 'he was excited to meet us' when you texted me on Saturday. How were you going to pull that off?" Jeremy asked. At that moment, the cocktail waitress came by.

"Another round of Dark & Stormy's?"

"Yeah. Keep 'em coming!" Brandy exclaimed. She turned her attention back to the guys. "So yeah...me and my big mouth and bright ideas. So you remember that night at the bar when I disappeared? Well, I went over to The Bungalow and sat at the bar. Ended up chatting...well, spilling all my guts to the guy next to me." She covered her face with her hands. Then continued, "So after our convo, he decided he could show up and play the role for the evening."

"And..." "Well, let's see. I ended up falling for him, but then realized he had a live-in girlfriend so....yeah. Here we are. Cheers!" Brandy said as she clinked her glass against theirs.

"Damn, Brandy. That's a lot. But seriously though. You didn't deserve that guy lying to you like that."

"Thanks. I mean, he said she was moving out, but whatever. I think I'm going to be off dating until the new year!"

The usual suspects from Bliss Bay started to trickle in. Hugs and well wishes were exchanged. Then Melissa arrived. Solo. Brandy found out that Kelly wasn't feeling well so she and Justin decided to skip the event.

So I did all this for nothing? Well, at least I told Matt and Jeremy. Brandy could finally breathe and enjoy herself. She was feeling good. At peace.

On her way back from a trip to the bathroom, she did a double take as she looked out the window. *Wait. Is that...Jalen? What is he doing here? I already told him I didn't need him anymore.*

At that moment, he saw her too. His eyes said he was sorry. He broke her gaze and then she saw him appear at the doorway where a bouncer was checking IDs. She walked up.

"Jalen, what are you doing here?" Brandy said shocked.

"I couldn't just let things end like that, Brandy. I know I should have mentioned Noelle, but I wasn't lying when I said we weren't together and she really is moving out. I know this started out as just a fun thing, but... I've really fallen for you."

Brandy grabbed Jalen and squeezed him tight! "I've fallen for you, too!" They stayed in their embrace for a moment before Brandy pulled away. "Come on and meet my friends...boyfrie nd!"

Epilogue
Danielle

How did I get here? Danielle wondered, metaphorically, as she looked out of the cab window and up at the Empire State Building lit up in purple. In an alternate universe, Danielle was curled up on the couch watching a scary movie with Marcus. In reality, she'd hopped on Amtrak on a whim to come to her best friend Brandy's Boos & Booze Halloween Party - the first event Brandy and her new boo, Jalen, were hosting together at his place in Brooklyn. After seeing how truly happy and cherished Brandy was in this new relationship, Danielle realized something was missing in hers. If you could call it that. It was definitely more of a situationship than a relationship for starters.

Marcus had been her on again, off again, friend with benefits for the past six years. But six hours ago, Danielle decided enough was enough and cut things off. Ultimately, she knew she deserved better than accepting the crumbs she'd been letting herself settle for. Eventually. She needed a break first. She decided to swear off men until at least the new year! But in the meantime, she needed a distraction. She called Brandy.

"Hey B?" she asked.

"Hey D. What's up?" Danielle could hear the sounds of a bustling bodega in the background. Brandy must have been doing last minute shopping for the party.

"Well, actually. I was wondering if you had room for one more at this party later. I cut things off with Marcus and need a distraction."

"For real?! Damn, D. That's a big deal. But I'm not surprised. You deserved better. You okay?"

"Yeah. I know. And I will be."

"Aww. Yeah! Come on up! And plenty of J's friends will be here, so maybe there will be a love connection. Heyyyy!" Brandy exclaimed.

Danielle smiled. Brandy was love struck! She was normally much more pragmatic than romantic, but Jalen had her spellbound. And planning on matching costumes. As Beyonce and Jay-Z, of course!

And so here she was. In a cab. On the way to a party of mostly strangers. Regretting her hasty choice to put on this sexy cat costume under her trench coat. It was uncomfortable trying to sit with this damn tail! She knew the party would have started by the time she arrived, so she decided to save time and just wear the costume.

A few minutes later she was buzzing to be let into the party. As she walked through the door she heard, "Can you hold the door, please?" from a deep voice behind her.

"Thanks!" the voice said as he walked in behind her. "You headed to the party, too?"

"Yeah," she said, as she finally took a good look at the guy. He had a fake black eye and a black shirt with a 'P' on it. "Wait. Are you a black-eyed pea?"

"Yup!" he replied, looking proud. "You are ....Inspector Gadget?" he asked as they began walking up the stairs.

She chuckled at his corniness. But she did kind of look like Inspector Gadget with this trench. "Nope. A cat," she explained as she opened up the coat and revealed her leopard print leotard. "It was last minute."

"No. It looks good," he replied as they approached the door. Danielle, in her "I'm over men" state, completely missed how this guy's eyes went wide at the sight of her tiny waist and toned legs. "I'm Andrew, by the way." He held out a hand.

"Danielle," she replied, shaking it back.

The moment was interrupted by the door to Jalen's apartment opening and the sounds of "Thriller" greeting them. They disappeared into the party. Andrew migrated toward the bar set up in the kitchen and Danielle made a beeline for Brandy.

The party was bustling. The music was bumping, the drinks were flowing, and a constant stream of people were in and out, mixing and mingling. Danielle did her best to interact despite knowing so few people and truly hating small talk. But it did give her something to do to keep her mind off Marcus and to give Brandy some room to host without her being glued to her side the entire night.

Like she often did when she was in situations where she felt awkward or out of place, she made it a game in her head. She would challenge her inner Oprah. *Okay. What can I learn besides somebody's job? How many people can I get to give me a real story?*

By the end of the night, she'd collected a few. She learned about one woman's out of body experience with the Running of the Bulls after asking about her all white attire accented by a red sash and scarf. She'd added a few books to her GoodReads list after a conversation with a guy dressed like "pumpkin pi" who was a Ph.D. student in history. She even got the juicy news that one of the women was knocked up! Danielle was minding her business pouring some bourbon into a red cup when she noticed the woman pouring her beer out of the bottle and into a cup and then replacing the contents with seltzer.

"Does that beer suck that bad?" Danielle joked.

The woman got wide eyed and looked over her shoulder before whispering, "Shhh. Not everyone knows yet, but I'm pregnant!"

"Congratulations!" Danielle whispered back. "Our secret."

She was happy to pass some of the time chatting with Brandy's older cousin, Gabby and her boyfriend, Dev, who were dressed like Catwoman and Batman. She and Brandy always thought Gabby's life was #goals. She was a successful entertainment lawyer, with a badass apartment, epic shoe collection, and hot boyfriend. A romantic at heart, Gabby always believed in happy endings. She left Danielle with some parting words about true love being right around the corner. Danielle sure hoped it would be.

Before long, most of the guests were trickling out of the party onto the streets of Brooklyn. Brandy was staying at Jalen's for the night. She offered Danielle a spot on his couch, but Danielle opted to take her best friend's keys and crash up at Brandy's place.

"I will be back in the morning and we can chat over brunch, okay, D?" Brandy said, taking Danielle's hand in hers.

"Sounds good, B. Love you!" she said, giving Brandy a big hug.

"Don't forget to text me when you get in!" Brandy shouted after her.

In the entryway of Jalen's building, Danielle waited on her Uber. *Really? It said 3 minutes 5 minutes ago!* She impatiently waited. She couldn't wait to get out of these boots. While she was waiting, Andrew came down the steps shortly after.

"Damn," she overheard him mutter. "22 minutes!"

"Uber times?" she asked. "Yeah. Mine was supposed to be here in 3 minutes," she said using air quotes. "But here we are 7 minutes later."

"You live nearby?" he asked.

"No, actually. I live in Baltimore. I'm just heading uptown to Brandy's to stay the night."

"Oh okay. Yeah, Brandy's cool. I met her at the beach last summer. I'm not sure if you know Jeremy from the house, but he's a buddy of mine."

Danielle looked down at her app. The Uber driver canceled.

"For real!" she muttered. "My Uber canceled. Guess I am staying here after all."

"Where are you headed?" Andrew asked.

"Upper West," Danielle informed him.

"Why don't you hop in with me? If you don't mind waiting..." he looked down at his phone. "Seven minutes. I can add a stop."

"Don't go out of your way. It's really fine."

"It's really no bother."

"Okay, thanks."

Danielle was tired and not thrilled about having to keep making small talk with this guy, but she did want to get to Brandy's. He was nice enough, but she was emotionally zapped.

"You been out to Bliss Bay at all?" Andrew asked.

"I haven't actually. Brandy talks about how great it is all the time though. I need to," Danielle responded.

She did really need to though. She'd hesitated because, honestly, even though Brandy was her best friend in the whole world, they had some differences in their upbringings and friend groups. Brandy grew up in a middle class, suburban New Jersey town and had spent a lot of time with her white friends and in white spaces. Danielle grew up in a working class Maryland town surrounded mostly by other

Black folks. She knew Brandy's Bliss Bay crew was mostly white, but hey. She somehow met Jalen out there so maybe Danielle could be a bit more open.

"Finally! Uber's here," Andrew stated. Danielle followed him out and into the car. When they were in the car, he asked, "So, Danielle, where does your costume rank in your all time top Halloween costumes?"

Well, that was better than the usual, 'What do you do for work?' questions most folks ask. "Eh. Middle of the road. I came up here last minute and it was the first thing I could find. I think the all time best was when Brandy and I were Salt-n-Pepa in college!"

"That's a good one. The important question though...did you have a Spinderella?" he asked.

Danielle was caught off guard for a beat. What did this seemingly basic white boy know about Spinderella?

"We did not."

"Ok, ok."

"What about you? Is this your best costume?"

"Nah. I think Clark Kent was the best. I mean, maybe a little too on the nose since I'm a journalist," Andrew said.

"Oh really. What type?" Danielle inquired.

"Economics reporter. Trust me. It's more exciting than it sounds."

"Oh I know. I'm in journalism, too. Content Editor for my local NPR."

"Nice! What made you choose radio?"

Before Danielle could answer, the car came to a halt on the Manhattan Bridge.

"Looks like an accident. GPS is saying at least 30 minutes until we get off the bridge," the driver said.

Danielle let out a sigh. Andrew was a little corny, but a good conversationalist, so Danielle didn't mind talking, but she also was exhausted and had only mentally prepared to keep up a conversation for a short time. She looked down at her phone hoping that she could amuse herself a bit with a game or scrolling social media as the conversation lulled.

Ugh. 12%.

And, of course, in the rush she didn't put her backup charger in her bag. And this wasn't one of those fancy Ubers with chargers. Looks like she was going to have to keep chatting with this Andrew guy after all....

***

What will happen next? Find out in the next book in the Bliss Bay Romance Series, *Danielle*, now available!

About the Author

Kayla has been writing since she could put a pen in her hand. While she's mostly written non-fiction, she's excited to venture into the Bliss Bay series as her first works of fiction. Her goal is to write compelling stories that center women of color.

Like her character, Brandy, Kayla was born and bred in New Jersey, loves spending time at the beach, eating bacon, and drinking black coffee and Cabernet Franc.

About Corner of Press (and Give them Romance)

Corner of Press is a small and independent publishing house for and by BIPOC women. Founded by two long time friends and writers, Krista Purnell and Sujeiry Gonzalez, Corner of Press publishes romance novels, poetry, memoir, and anthologies that celebrate the Black and Latinx experience through creative storytelling.

Representation matters as does celebrating and sharing BIPOC stories that incite joy and laughter. We are not here to highlight our struggle, we are here to shine our light.

Keep in Touch

Website: https://givethemromance.com

Facebook: https://www.facebook.com/givethemromance

Instagram: https://www.instagram.com/givethemromance

TikTok: https://www.tiktok.com/@givethemromancebooks